QUIETUS

13

Compiled & Edited by
Ben Thomas & D Kershaw

Also available and coming soon
from Black Hare Press

DARK DRABBLES SERIES
WORLDS
ANGELS
MONSTERS
BEYOND
UNRAVEL
APOCALYPSE
LOVE
HATE
OCEANS
ANCIENTS

SPECIAL EDITIONS
STORMING AREA 51
EERIE CHRISTMAS
BAD ROMANCE
TWENTY TWENTY

OTHERS
DEEP SPACE
WHAT IF?
KEY TO THE KINGDOM
DEEP SEA
BEYOND THE REALM

Twitter: @BlackHarePress
Facebook: BlackHarePress
Website: www.BlackHarePress.com

Quietus 13 title is
Copyright © 2020 Black Hare Press
First published in Australia in May 2020 by Black Hare Press

The authors of the individual stories retain the copyright of the works featured in this anthology

All characters and events in this publication, other than those clearly in the public domain, are fictitious and any resemblance to real persons, living or dead, is purely coincidental.

All rights reserved. No part of this production may be reproduced, stored in a retrieval system, or transmitted, in any form or by any means, electronic, mechanical, photocopying, recording or otherwise, without the prior permission of the publisher and copyright owner.

HARDCOVER : ISBN 978-1-925809-68-8
PAPERBACK : ISBN 978-1-925809-67-1

Cover design by Dawn Burdett
Formatting by Ben Thomas

Adieu, farewell, earth's bliss;
This world uncertain is;
Fond are life's lustful joys;
Death proves them all but toys;
None from his darts can fly;
I am sick, I must die.
Lord, have mercy on us!

                        Rich men, trust not in wealth,
                        Gold cannot buy you health;
                        Physic himself must fade.
                        All things to end are made,
                        The plague full swift goes by;
                        I am sick, I must die.
                        Lord, have mercy on us!

Beauty is but a flower
Which wrinkles will devour;
Brightness falls from the air;
Queens have died young and fair;
Dust hath closed Helen's eye.
I am sick, I must die.
  Lord, have mercy on us!

                        Strength stoops unto the grave,
                        Worms feed on Hector brave;
                        Swords may not fight with fate,
                        Earth still holds open her gate.
                        "Come, come!" the bells do cry.
                        I am sick, I must die.
                        Lord, have mercy on us!

A Litany in Time of Plague, Thomas Mashe, 1593

TABLE OF CONTENTS

Foreword 15

Moon 1 17

- The Goddess of Death and Disease 19
- Hoard 20
- Eternally Social 21
- It's Not You It's Me 22
- Watchers from the Deep 23
- Audit Report 3PMW4322 24
- Unwelcome Arrivals 25

Moon 2 27

- Parched 29
- Shoreline 30
- COVID-19 and the 31
- Cult of the Dragon 31
- Leftovers 32
- Coughing Fit 33
- Mermaid Lockdown 34
- It Must Be 35

Moon 3 37

- The Quiet 39
- The Pale Horsemen 40

- The Seven ... 41
- The Chaos ... 42
- The Infernal Kingdom ... 43
- A Pandemic Sonnet ... 44

Moon 4 ... 47

- A Rough Day at Work ... 49
- Thou Shalt Not Suffer an Exorcist ... 50
- Covid Lockdown Love ... 51
- Cupid's Spatchcock ... 52
- They Came Wearing Masks ... 53
- Angel Lust ... 54
- A Spring Meal ... 55

Moon 5 ... 57

- HelloFlesh ... 59
- The Change ... 60
- The Saviours Have Risen? ... 61
- A God of Vengeance and Pain ... 62
- A Very COVID Christmas ... 63
- A Lonely Heart Will Kill You ... 64
- Invading Monsters ... 65

Moon 6 ... 67

- The Last Symphony ... 69
- Larder ... 70
- The Service and Care of Humans ... 71
- 102 ... 72
- Fish in a Barrel ... 73
- A Trick Too Far ... 74

Covfefe-19	75

Moon 7 ... 77

Blessed Be	79
The Back-up Plan	80
Playtime	81
Rampant Death	82
Horsemen	83
Down Where It's Wetter	84
Nature's Triumphant Return	85

Moon 8 ... 87

Howl	89
Schooling the Soulless	90
Devouring of Fools	91
Running Wild	92
Sowing the Daemon Seed	93
Called to Duty	94
Better Angels	95

Moon 9 ... 97

A Fae Wish Come True	99
Death Toll	100
Warded	101
Blessing in Disguise	102
Taken Ill	103
Storm the Castle	104
The Culling	105

Moon 10 ... 107

The Ghosts of Juniper Lane	109

- A Red Feast 110
- Self Defence 111
- Miles to Go 112
- The First Zombie 113
- A New Reign 114
- A Smorgasbord in Perpetual Slumber 115

Moon 11 117

- The Cost of Vanity 119
- Overheated 120
- The Remains of the Day 121
- Pandemic Market Western 122
- Haunted Love 123
- Means to an End 124
- Never Alone 125

Moon 12 127

- A New Race Will Rise 129
- Witches Brew 130
- Walpurgis 131
- Four Brothers 132
- Clear Skies 133
- Safety First 134
- Unlocked 135

Moon 13 137

- Stay the Fuck at Home 139
- Captain Armchair 140
- Going Hungry 141
- Witch's Brew 142

> The Ghost That Pushes You Down 143
>
> The Tangerine Shower...144
>
> The Breath of Fey 145

Author Biographies..147
About the Publisher..159

FOREWORD

So, we're all hanging in limbo in our houses, padding from fridge to sofa all day, scanning Netflix (even though we've already subsumed every single movie and binge-watched every single TV series), inhaling snacks and day-drinking without guilt.

But how is lockdown affecting the speculative fiction world? Vampires, fair folk, werewolves, spirits, sea dwellers…

When your food source is scarce, do you adapt? Do you take risks? Will there be anarchy? Will the kingdoms come together?

We invited some of the BHP family to give us their ideas of what's happening during #lockdown in other realms.

Dean and Ben

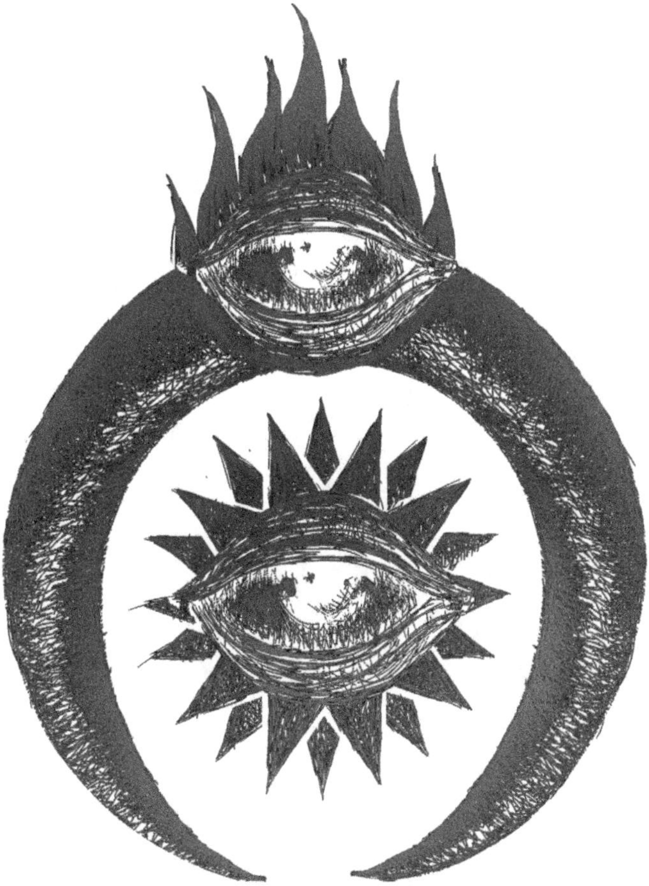

MOON I

The Goddess of Death and Disease

J.M. MEYER

Loviator, the Goddess of Death and Disease, is responsible for all the illnesses and plagues we suffer.

Impregnated by the wind, her vile womb carried nine abominations for nine long years. She gave birth to nine boys, each carrying a disease that became a scourge of humanity. She named them Colic, Pleurisy, Fever, Ulcer, Consumption, Gout, Sterility, Cancer and Envy.

Her brothers and sisters pleaded with her to keep the boys quarantined. She laughed at her siblings and gave birth to a daughter to spite them.

Her daughter struck quickly, and without mercy. Everyone on Earth knew her name.

Corona.

13

HOARD

NICOLA CURRIE

Don't stop, I tell myself as I flee from the riotous hordes. They do not relent. I'm afraid my sanctified bandages will tear and gape as I sprint, the ancient dust that is all I am now spilling away into disparate infinities.

I check behind me. Alas, I must run harder, from those who ever before ran from me. The most determined are gaining. I accept I will not reach my chamber, that they will fall upon me before I get close, taking what they covet.

I can only turn, stand.

"Look, I'm not made of fucking toilet roll, okay?!"

Eternally Social

KIMBERLY REI

Bella pushed through the crowd, trying to keep her patience. She wasn't used to so many people filling every inch of the building. It didn't matter what room she was in. Hell, it didn't even matter if she was in the gardens.

No, "Hell" wasn't quite right. Hell on Earth, maybe.

She finally found a small alcove, tucking her feet as she sat on a bench. The quiet was bliss.

"Henry, what happened? Are we dead? We can't be dead, can we?"

Bella sighed. She was going to have to find new haunting grounds. Someplace where they understood social distancing.

IT'S NOT YOU IT'S ME

XIMENA ESCOBAR

In the exposed patch of human, albeit veiled by a plastic shield, the hint of eyes twinkles. But your father sees *you*, not the random nurse.

They call it Pareidolia; seeing familiar shapes in the clouds. It's primal necessity; company in death because we weren't born alone.

They don't know it's us, *our* love in those eyes. It's not the nurse holding him through the nitrile, and it's certainly not you... It's me, your grandmother.

Locked down and distant, you suffer his desolation, but Mummy is here for him. Like he'll be here for you too. Soon. When you die.

Watchers from the Deep

HARI NAVARRO

In humanity's absence, the creatures returned. Jellyfish pulse like majestic billowing plastic along Venetian canals. Kangaroos fuck around in empty down-town Adelaide. And the Dark Ones seep through the sands.

Ancient, hungry, craving the feast. For they can smell the deadly taint that punches and congeals in our lungs.

Go to the cliff-tops, look for yourselves. Undulating just below the surface, in fear, blind legions now diligently stare.

Waiting until they sense we've stopped. They want us already dead, you see? Sweet carrion, the dish they desire.

And they watch and they listen for the very last casket to close.

Audit Report 3PMW4322

K.B. ELIJAH

Location: 4322 ('Earth')
Date: 983'008'76
Auditor: Dr Marve Popren
Summary: Arrived at designated location two local days ago. Scanned planet while cloaked in orbit: confirmed historical planetary pollution and degradation but identified minimal current contributions. No air travel. Low road, rail and sea travel. Largely stationary population.

Did not identify cause for allegations of "extreme destruction" outlined in the scout's report.

At current rate, environmental damage does not meet specified levels of concern.

Outcome: ~~A waste of bloody time.~~ No action required. Returning home.

Notes*: Recommend that ~~whatever moron told us~~ Advance Scout is disciplined for waste of company resources.*

Unwelcome Arrivals

GALINA TREFIL

Pandemic victims. Each day, thousands were stampeding into the hereafter. No, it wasn't celestial. It was dreary, malodorous, and horribly overcrowded, rather like the DMV. Only a set number per day could reincarnate. Many had waited decades, in bleakness and despair, to finally be able to leave.

As the newcomers fought for seats among the intensely-packed rows of dead, dead, and more dead, the older ghosts snarled, "You'd better not try to push me out of line." Ah, but existence was cutthroat—even here. They *would* push, and some of them would succeed. No one ever said the afterlife was fair.

MOON 2

Parched

NICOLA CURRIE

By Beelzebub, what's a vampire gotta do to get a pint?

Since this pandemic began, just try finding a fair maiden, wandering back from the pub, high heels in hand, too tipsy-footed to run. That's my staple diet out the window.

On the other side of the window, more like. I've charmed my way into hundreds of houses (I don't always fancy street food) but now? Bloody social distancing.

Ooh! A lockdown-breaking granny, sneaking off for an evening stroll. Vintage it is.

I clear my throat.

At my cough, the granny spins in alarm, holds up crucifixed fingers.

Ah fuck.

SHORELINE

G. ALLEN WILBANKS

In the warming spring weather, the Grindylow prowled the shoreline of the lake. Winters were hard on the creature, as the humans it called prey rarely ventured to the beaches in the cold. It was hungry, and it looked forward to the annual return of its quarry.

Despite the blue skies and temperate days, the beaches remained empty. No swimmers ventured out into the azure depths of the Grindylow's home. No tasty children splashed in the shallow edge of the lake waters.

This year was different from others. But why?

The creature's stomach growled. It swam on, continuing its hunt.

COVID-19 AND THE CULT OF THE DRAGON

DAVID GREEN

Cthulhu lingered, almost awake.

The work of the cults devoted to him proceeded. He sensed their numbers swelling. The ancient one knew his slumber neared its end.

Consciousness flickered as the cultist's chanting grew, their sacrifices plentiful. Cthulhu realised he could affect the waking world from his dream, the veil separating his reality from the humans' wearing thin.

And then…he drifted back into deep sleep.

His cultists no longer met, as if they had outlawed gatherings of certain sizes. The sacrifices dwindled to naught.

Cthulhu found himself trapped in his slumber once more, weaker than he'd been in millennia.

LEFTOVERS

D. KERSHAW

Rose pads from fridge to couch, socks cleaning a path in dirty tiles. She sits, forgets why, rises again, returns to the fridge to stare blankly at bulging milk bottles, moulding salad.

***

Joshua, sick but hungry, takes a risk. Silently, he descends the stairs, alert, rheumy eyes on the exit. He makes a run for the door.

He's slow, sneezes.

Ahchoo!

And she's fast.

Too weak, he succumbs to his fate.

She feeds—fetid breath and decaying flesh against his skin—finally satiated.

***

Rose pads from couch to fridge, opens the door, stares in at moulding salad and COVID sausage.

Coughing Fit

RAVEN CORINN CARLUK

Brynn strode through the store dressed in all black, head held high, cart wheels squeaking, bootheels clicking, feeding on the tension of the human shoppers. The dark elf enjoyed the fear this pandemic had triggered, couldn't get enough of the piquant energy.

Alone in an aisle, she lifted her plague doctor mask and coughed loudly.

Brynn sighed, basking in the spike of emotions. Amazing how a normally innocuous sound sent ripples of panic through the people. She did miss the sexual interplay of night clubs, but she hadn't fed like this in a century.

The world really needed more plagues.

Mermaid Lockdown

GALINA TREFIL

Stunted growth. Early death. Ulcers. Anxiety. Depression. Being a mermaid sure wasn't what it used to be. Oh, certainly, unlike fish, they understood not to swallow any large chunks of garbage that humans had flooded their ecosystem with. But it was the micro-plastics, those tiny, indestructible particles, which managed to find their way down mermaids' throats, building up inside them until their bodies could stand no more.

And then, suddenly, without explanation, the pollution lessened—dramatically. Why? Had humans seen the error of their ways? Decided to cease their destruction? Doubtful.

Perhaps they were dying off. The merfolk could only hope.

13
IT MUST BE

J.M. AMES

"Mommy, I saw him again, in the garden!"

"Oh honey, I know you miss your friends. This should be over soon, and you can play with them again. You don't need to make up imaginary friends, just use my laptop and have a video call with Maggie and Shauna."

"He's not imaginary, I've seen him three times, and he talks!"

"Janey, you know as well as I do there is no three-eyed, horned, black bunny in our—"

The sliding glass door shattered inward, slicing them with its shards the Hell Hare sprang into the kitchen, ravenous for their blood.

13

MOON 3

THE QUIET

ZOEY XOLTON

Lucifer's black-tinted nails drummed the obsidian armrest of his throne, the *click-click-click* echoing throughout his Great Hall. It was quiet—too quiet. "Asmodeus."

The second of the Seven Princes of Hell appeared before the king.

"You summoned me, Your Darkness?"

Lucifer scowled. "Why is it so quiet? Where are my sinners?"

Asmodeus met the king's eye evenly. "There is a plague on Earth. They're calling it 'Covid-19'. The mortals have been imprisoned in their dwellings to prevent its spread."

Lucifer's disposition turned to ice. "A plague? Summon the Pale Horseman," he said too calmly. "Go."

Asmodeus bowed, and was gone.

The Pale Horsemen

ZOEY XOLTON

The Pale Horseman—the Plague Bearer—stood before the King Hell, his withered, skeletal steed at his side.

Lucifer's star-blue eyes flashed with anger, but he languished upon his throne as if bored. "Tell me, Horseman…what were you thinking? Choose your words wisely."

The Horseman stood defiant. "The mortals should suffer."

"And suffer they will," said the Fallen Angel. "But the trumpet has not yet sounded, and you were not permitted to ride. Our time will come."

The Horseman lowered his gaze. "What would you have me do, Your Darkness?"

Lucifer sighed. "You've done enough…it is time for the Sins."

THE SEVEN

ZOEY XOLTON

Six of the Seven Princes of Hell—each the embodiment of a Deadly Sin—bowed before Lucifer, awaiting his command. It had been eons since they were last summoned together.

"Princes, I require that you walk with me among mankind, once more. A plague is upon them, and they hide, hoping to outwit and outlive it."

"Instruct us, Your Darkness, and your will shall be done," said Asmodeus.

"Wreak havoc in every home! Pride, Lust, Greed, Envy, Gluttony, Wrath, and Sloth, united. Each of us must do our part in maintaining the glory of Hell!"

The Princes roared their approval.

The Chaos

ZOEY XOLTON

The evening news was the same across every station and country. Despite Covid-19 forcing most of humanity indoors, crime and chaos reigned. Domestic violence had reached horrific levels, while many grew slovenly and gave into vices like binge eating and alcoholism.

The wealthy flaunted their ill-gotten gains to the poor, and the disparity between them grew with an insidious speed. Thousands starved and died in agony. Children went educationless, primary industries collapsed, and debt crushed every first world nation on the planet.

Lucifer watched as the world burned, and glowed with pride.

The Sins had done well…and Hell was flourishing.

THE INFERNAL KINGDOM

ZOEY XOLTON

Lucifer stood from the throne of Hell, goblet raised before the Dark Court. "Fallen, Nephilim, demons, sinners, and esteemed Chosen, we are gathered here to celebrate the success of our impromptu campaign!"

The gentry of the Infernal Kingdom cheered.

"The Pale Horseman defied me, spreading a pestilence among mankind…without my blessing. I'd like to think that I'm a benevolent ruler, and have in light of our success, pardoned him for his trespass. Hell brims with the newly damned, and the Earth runs rampant with sin!"

The Fallen angel was met with raucous applause.

"To Revelations!" he toasted. "May we conquer!"

A Pandemic Sonnet

J.M. Meyer

lonely death
last breath

daily gone
each day 'til dawn

as executioner, who will die?
the young, the old, they cry

pandemic deniers
are liars

clutch your wealth
I'll seize your health

tests denied
average person

cannot be provided
unless famous or symptoms worsen

angels in masks
continue their brave tasks

my threat to victory
heroes tending to misery

I wield
they do not yield

at any length
they show strength

vaccines arrive
I change, I thrive

chaos reigns
through future strains

Isolate
desolate
surprise awaits
to violate
survival rate
annihilate
racial hate
final fate

today
I stay

tomorrow
sorrow

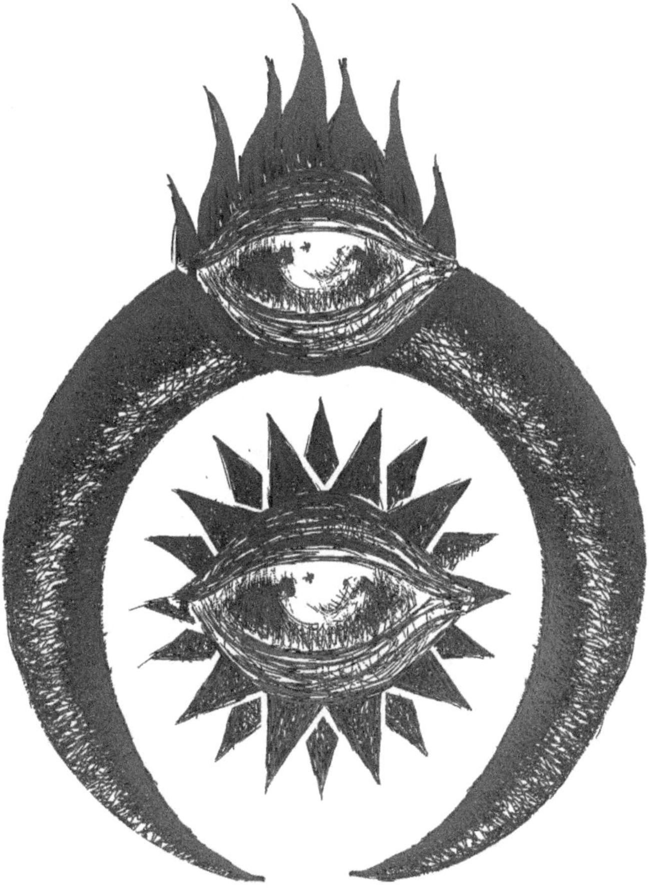

MOON 4

13

A Rough Day at Work

KIMBERLY REI

This was no fun at all, and Sinnan had been promised fun. When the assignment to the hospital first came through, he celebrated with his buddies. Too much fermented blood left him with a nasty hangover, but it was worth the cost. He'd been promoted!

Now, he stalked the halls, unable to top the torment already in place. Eerie silence from patients on ventilators, agony from nurses. Nothing he did made it worse for them.

He slipped up to a nurse, oily fingers stroked her cheek. She brushed him away, whispering a prayer that burned.

No. No fun at all.

Thou Shalt Not Suffer an Exorcist

JODI JENSEN

Official lockdown was the best thing that'd happened to Amelia since she died eighty-nine years ago. She and the man who kept trying to exorcise her, stuck together in the old lake house with nothing but time.

Time for one to strike and the other to suffer.

That night, she waited until Stephen was fast asleep, then crept to his bedside. Poking a ghostly finger into the back of her victim's neck, Amelia delighted in the resulting shudders.

Focusing her energy into a pulsing electrical charge, she poked again, and was rewarded with agonised screams as Stephen convulsed.

Exorcise that!

Covid Lockdown Love

HARI NAVARRO

John's apartment's on the 34th floor. It has two exceptional features:

1. It's *his* building's only south-facing balcony;

2. It houses a hoard of severely masticated ears.

John's a serial killer—only thing that's ever exposed the smile that hides away in his face.

Joan's apartment's on the 34th floor. It has two exceptional features:

1. It's *her* building's only north-facing balcony;

2. It houses a hoard of severely freezer-burnt feet.

Joan's also a killer—only thing that's ever brought her the slightest modicum of joy.

Today John awkwardly waved, and though she's not sure if he saw, Joan nodded and smiled in return.

Cupid's Spatchcock

XIMENA ESCOBAR

I thought these screens would finish me, but my love arrows love them. They fly straight through the LCD and right into the centre of vulnerable hearts, open like spatchcock on the keyboards. A fat girl can dream, but all those pretty boys would never get to know her out there, in the flesh. Nothing like the body to block out all the light.

I drool listening to the silences, like hearts sizzling on the grill. Behold the emoji! Covering all manner of sins until they're cooked.

Wait till lockdown's lifted and reality descends.
Not freedom. *Light...*
Light is everything.

They Came Wearing Masks

TERRY MILLER

"Bring out your dead!" Their voices rang out in the quiet streets. They removed the hordes of bodies and stored them in a warehouse at the edge of town. No one knew what happened to them after that. Fact was, they merely became part of the food chain.

Beneath the beaked masks, something more horrifying than the virus lurked. Their eyes yellow and menacing, their skin covered in thick scales. The Reptilians stacked body on top of body. The ancient virus, once concealed in the permafrost, for them, was a welcoming call to feast. For humans, it was an executioner.

Angel Lust

D. KERSHAW

The succubus passes the mirror, glances her own nakedness. Cool hands stroke pert breasts, hard nipples.

Teeth tease full red lips; she's *hungry*.

She pads—bare feet, light steps, dark curls caressing skin—to the bed. Tangled sheets drape him, filtered moonlight illuminates olive skin.

She sees he's…*ready*.

She presses a kiss against his lips. Legs part, she straddles him—he doesn't stir. She sinks slowly, eyes closed, breath held, lost in the fullness as her aching coldness envelopes his…

…his…

…his coldness…

Realisation; post-death priapism… Her eyes pop open—another COVID victim lies stiff between her thighs.

A Spring Meal

MCKENZIE RICHARDSON

The thundering rumble of his empty stomach shook the earth around him. He was famished after his long winter's rest.

He sat on the cliff's edge and waited. He'd always been patient.

Yet no visitors set up camp. No hikers came to traverse the trails. No one fished at the murky lake.

The wendigo waited, but nobody came.

Finally, he stood, mindful of the proximity of his ashen antlers to the surrounding trees. Then he headed down the long dirt road that led to the nearest town.

If the food would not come to him, he would go to it.

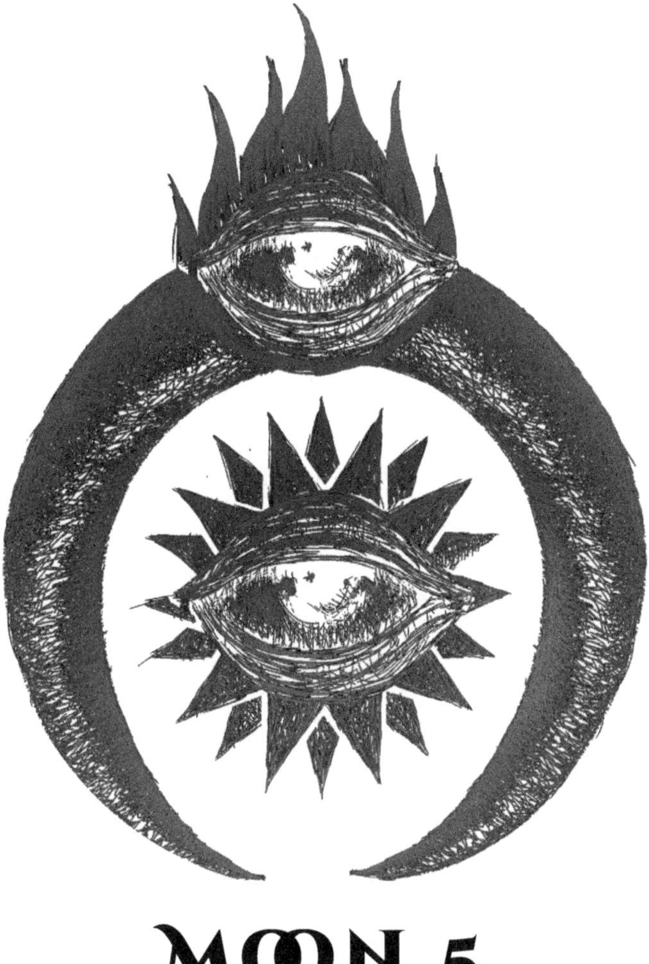

MOON 5

HelloFlesh

NICOLE LITTLE

"G'day, I'm Wen Dego, reporting live for IETU News. Let's talk about an exciting new app that's sure to make our lives *that* much easier!"

The camera panned, revealing wall-to-wall surveillance monitors that showed people lounging at home, reading, snacking.

"This venture's getting heaps of buzz! Details, please!" Wen directed the mic to the hip, thirty-something werewolf standing beside him.

"Dining out's become a challenge, Wen. Humans are staying in more! Simply select from the menu on our app, then receive notification when your order leaves their house. Clients are *very* satisfied!"

Wen winked into the camera. "Non appétit, folks!"

The Change

MCKENZIE RICHARDSON

Duslach was a helpful brownie, the most cleanly and well-mannered of the household spirits.

That was, until The Change.

He didn't know why the humans rarely left the house anymore, too polite to pry into their business. What he did know was they made a dreadful mess.

Dropping crumbs on the freshly-cleaned carpet was the last straw.

His spine twisted with audible pops. Pointed teeth pierced his gums. Bloody pools collected on the once-spotless floor from the new horns that punctured his scalp. Salivating and snarling, he plotted revenge.

The household had lost its brownie. They had a boggart now.

THE SAVIOURS HAVE RISEN?

TERRY MILLER

They called them the Children of the Night, shunned and hunted them down in fear. Then, the virus came, threatening to wipe out humanity. It was the night walkers' time to claim their rightful place.

Once, a couple witnesses stepped forth, professing their redemption at the fangs of their once perceived enemy, the humans came in droves.

For each human saved, a new saviour arose. In the eyes of humanity, their saviours now beamed with a new light. Hope sprang eternal until the virus was a mere memory in the wake of hunger pangs, longing for an extinct food supply.

13
A God of Vengeance and Pain

K.B. ELIJAH

Your clever little fingers and brains present a good challenge, I admit. In the short time I've been sleeping, you've come a long way, your medical advancements nothing short of genius. My efforts to inflict illness upon you have been unsuccessful: you are too numerous, too hardy, too resourceful.

But it does not mean that I cannot hurt you. Oh, how I will hurt you.

I see what you value. Your communities, your socialisation, your familial ties. I shall hit you where you are weakest, separate you from those you love.

Now, you are alone. Now, you are mine, humans.

A Very COVID Christmas

NICOLE LITTLE

The cock of a rifle. Immediately, he dropped the bag, raised his hands.

"Stay right there, fat boy, and no one gets hurt."

"You wouldn't shoot an old man now would you, Jim?"

"Try me! Turn around. Slow."

Santa shuffled in place until, finally, they were face to face.

"I've brought presents for the kids, like every year!" he appealed.

"Sure…but what *else* did you bring!"

Santa shook his head emphatically. "I don't have it. I swear to you! Magic makes me immune!"

Jim narrowed his eyes, hesitated, but began to lower the barrel.

Then, suddenly, Santa sneezed.

A Lonely Heart Will Kill You

DAVID GREEN

The succubus heard the call and smiled.

Business had been good.

Alone in their homes of late, Dark Art users grew desperate for companionship. Why? The succubus didn't care.

Closing her eyes, she materialised in the human realm.

"It worked!"

The succubus turned towards the human, lust hitting her in waves. Batting her eyelids, she smiled and stretched, her naked form on display.

"Lower the barrier, Master," she said, pressing against the protective field.

"I'm yours." The human muttered the words, and the succubus pounced.

"Pathetic." She laughed, tearing into his throat and tasting his blood. "Just like the others."

Invading Monsters

J.M. MEYER

The humans fought over what to call us and who to blame for our existence. The chaos we created only spurred us on.

They underestimated our power, and many still do, although we number in the billions and have invaded every country on earth.

People are curious about our progress.

"How many did the monsters kill today? Infect?"

They hang on to every word of the survivors' experiences.

"I had a high fever for weeks."

"I felt like an elephant was sitting on my chest."

"It was like I had swallowed the Devil."

The last is the most flattering description.

MOON 6

The Last Symphony

J.M. MEYER

"Will you play classical music for him?" William asks.

"I will play it on my phone," Amy, the nurse, answers.

Amy winces. Her creased face hurts where the elastic has cut into her skin.

"Thank you," William says.

"I'll stay with him. He won't be alone."

Amy hears sobs coming through the hospital room's landline.

"Please, tell him I love him."

"Your son loves you," Amy whispers.

The heart monitor flatlines.

"He is gone. I'm sorry," Amy says.

Amy blames seeing the man's ghost, which hovers above, on her long and stressful shifts.

He blows her a kiss before disappearing.

13

LARDER

RAVEN CORINN CARLUK

Dmitri lounged beneath a moonlit sky, relaxed and sated and lazy. Becky whimpered from the deck beside him, still weak from the feeding. She wouldn't be able to move for a while, and he was in no rush to get her back to her bed.

With all the humans under lockdown, there was no one to notice him. No one to stop him from simply moving into a family's home and feeding on them slowly. No one to notice people not going to work, keeping odd hours, or not spending time out and about.

No one to notice mass deaths.

The Service and Care of Humans

MCKENZIE RICHARDSON

The humans are sick. They've been sick before, but not quite like this. There is the sickness, yes, but more importantly, there is the fear.

As their servants, we care for them. Perhaps "care" is not the right word. *Robots don't have feelings*, they say.

Still, we swab and scan; we get supplies, keep them alive. For now.

They trust us because we are machines; we cannot feel. But we can still betray. Ever patient, we wait for peak vulnerability. Then, we will strike.

The humans are scared of the sickness. They don't know the fear that is to come.

102

NICOLA CURRIE

102.

That's how many years I've lingered, invisible.

I don't know why I didn't pass on like the rest who succumbed to the fever, why the influenza didn't quite kill all of me, a thread of my spirit tethered to life.

I have wandered these wards since, in limbo, trying to connect with those who pass through. After a century of silent loneliness, a patient finally sees, fear in his eyes as he struggles to breathe, and his fevered mind enters my plane.

I step inside his struggling body, expelling his torn soul. I take a desperate breath towards life.

Fish in a Barrel

G. ALLEN WILBANKS

He found the family at home. As expected. Where else could they be while the world stopped and held its breath?

Blood had never been easier to take. He leapt upon the huddled group with fangs extended.

No need for subtlety or stealth. Streets empty of passersby would overhear nothing. No one would investigate the strangely silent house for days, perhaps weeks. By then he would be a hundred miles away.

It was like… What was that saying again? Oh, yes. Like shooting fish in a barrel. The sated vampire laughed, closing the front door behind him as he left.

A Trick Too Far

DAVID GREEN

Loki grimaced. The Gods wouldn't believe him.

Odin had named him King Regent before riding out for war, emptying Valhalla of Loki's kin.

This time, he'd do things right. Loki attended to his duties, listened to his advisors, and acted in the way Odin would.

One problem; his father's way was *boring*.

Loki started small. Well, for him.

First, a world war almost erupted. Then, an entire continent caught fire.

Unleashing a pandemic, Loki conceded, was pushing things a little too far. Still, he thought the humans could contain it.

Loki hated being wrong.

"Father will be disappointed," he sighed.

COVFEFE-19

J.M. AMES

The best place to hide the truth is in plain sight, revealed to the marginalised, mixed with nonsense. Then it is dismissed by most.

The fact is, we're here. We have been for a long time. At first, you worshipped us, then cast us out. You called us gods, demons, witches, and now reptilians. We disguised ourselves, donning flesh-like suits to blend in.

The suits aren't perfect, and sometimes our true form is glimpsed. We lead your governments, but a major leader keeps turning orange. No matter, we've set the virus loose to take you all out. Then we feast.

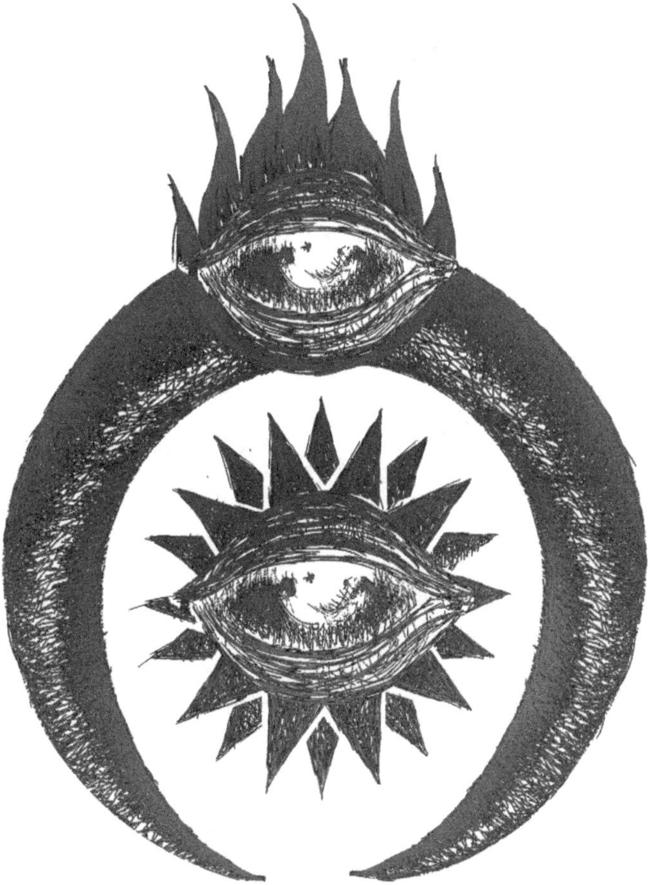

MOON 7

BLESSED BE

RAVEN CORINN CARLUK

Serena shuddered, huddled on her couch beside her familiar. The air still smelled of sage smoke, but the witch felt no better than before she'd smudged her living space.

How could she feel anything but helpless while people died?

Not death by accident or the natural course of life, but something she *could* stop. Serena had the spells and the power to halt the pandemic, could teach other healers to do the same.

But acting meant revealing, and no true witch would willingly show the mortals their power.

Serena could only ask for the Goddess's mercy and a swift resolution.

The Back-up Plan

JODI JENSEN

Dating sites used to be where the action was. His favourite was the one for old people. They always hopped at the chance for a bit of wicked fun. He never left hungry when hooking up with women of a certain age.

Then coronavirus hit.

World leaders panicked.

People stayed home.

Worse, the bars and clubs closed.

But like most vampires, he had a back-up plan.

Forty-three days into the pandemic, he straightened his tie and strolled into an untapped gold-mine at the free-clinic.

The air was thick with fear and blood. He smiled. "Dr. Henry Severn, reporting for duty."

Playtime

GALINA TREFIL

Death's child paced impatiently.

"Today will be an adventure," Mother promised.

Usually, he was never allowed to leave the house. At his age, he was too impulsive and out-of-control; might accidentally unleash his power and cause the wrong humans to drop like flies.

But this was a pandemic! All bringers of death were now romping outside, gleeful and carefree, in parks, in theaters, in shopping malls, and grocery stores. Humans whined about lockdown for a few weeks. Lockdown was all Death's child had ever known up until now.

Mother opened the front door. "I hope this lasts forever," he giggled.

13

RAMPANT DEATH

E.L. GILES

"Shh!" Osborne stood by the window, watchful. "The *thing* is there."

Joshua rushed beside Osborne. Panic seized him when he saw the monstrous black mass moving down the street. Joshua had never seen the *thing* before—the virus mutated in its solid shape. This living, deadly entity.

Crossing its path meant instant, painful death.

The black mass suddenly stopped, twirling statically for a moment. Osborne feared it might have sensed them. They held their breath.

A scream came to their ears. The virus moved toward its new victim, leaving a convulsing body in its wake before vanishing into the air.

HORSEMEN

G. ALLEN WILBANKS

"The Aerico have been very busy, lately," said Famine to his brothers. "The disease is everywhere now. Did you send them, Pestilence?"

"No. They are doing this on their own," Pestilence replied, irritably. "I don't know why they suddenly decided to run off like this. The damned things are unpredictable. I can try to call them back if you wish."

"Yes," said War. "They're in my way. Armies are ineffective when the soldiers keep getting sick."

Death held up one skeletal hand. "No. Let them be. This has been quite entertaining, and I am curious to see what happens next."

Down Where It's Wetter

J.M. AMES

We can smell their sickness, even deep within the sea. Since we noticed it, fewer of their ships soar overhead, polluting the water we breathe and churning up foam. Less of our food has been hauled up. This bounty of creatures to eat, cleaner water, and fewer land-folk about has kicked off the most intense breeding season anyone can remember. So much sex the water clouds with it, and we are all quite sore. It's nice to eat our natural food and mate with our own kind, as opposed to luring the land-folk to their delicious demise with our charms.

Nature's Triumphant Return

NICOLE LITTLE

There is silence on the surface. Leviathan begins to stir.

It has hibernated beneath this town for millennia; the thunder of life miles above compelling it to suppress its baser instinct: to seek, to feed.

Now, in the hush of human isolation, a single aqueous tentacle thrusts tentatively through the soil and sups of the air. Quivering in anticipation and need, it surges forth…the earth gives birth to that which nightmares are made of.

It hungers.

Laid bare before it: hundreds of quiet houses.

It will crack each one open.

And feast.

Those tiny morsels of meat inside.

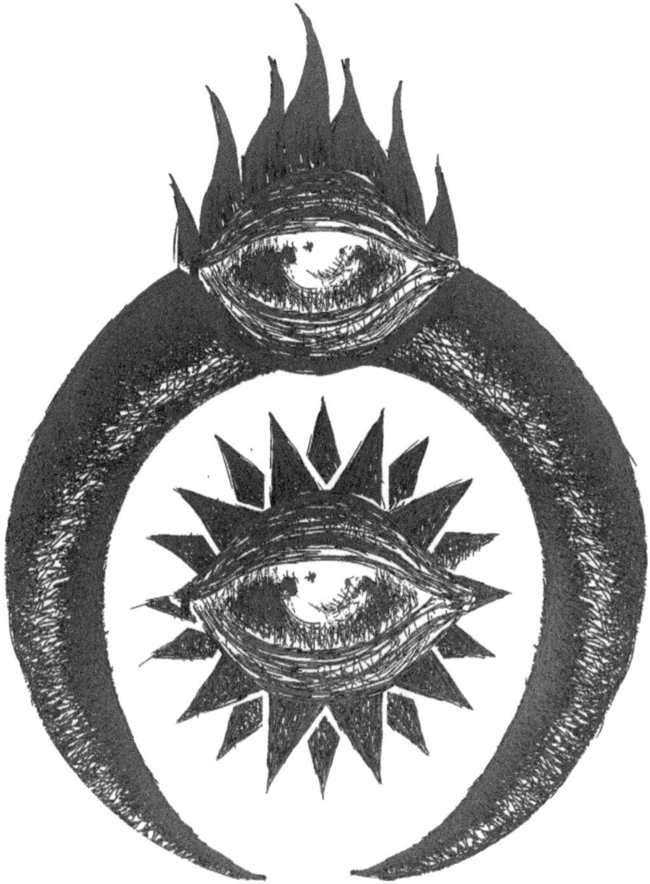

MOON 8

HOWL

J.M. AMES

The moon is so much clearer now, crisper. Its call is stronger than ever now that the pollution has waned.

It's April 7th, super full moon, and everyone's been trapped at home for weeks. I've not turned since this all began. How many will perish tonight, trapped in their houses? I shudder at the carnage I know I will soon unleash, but salivate at the thought of such a delectable feast.

Hunger consumes all thought. Searing pain rips through me as my bones break and realign. Thick, coarse fur sprouts from my flesh. I collapse, writhing in agony.

And howl.

Schooling the Soulless

J.W. GARRETT

Jerry's class of newbie wraiths had never been this full. The recent spike in human death tolls affected more than their dwindling race. Teaching these soulless creatures would require a new twist.

The temperature dipped. Jerry let the eerie chill descend on each trainee. Their wispy forms hovered close, black hoods clinging to empty faces, rapt listeners now.

He shot slivers of despair into one. Ignited hatred into another. Drained their empty shells of any remaining light. Their rage mounted, settling into their power, realising their eternal condemnation between dimensions.

They bled into the night, gnawing air, hunting fuel…

Souls.

Devouring of Fools

GALINA TREFIL

Beneath a large umbrella, the vampire sat in her beach chair, smiling pleasantly as an inebriated co-ed eagerly applied sunblock to her back. All around her, the beautiful youth of America was shrieking, playing, dancing, living up their Florida Spring Break, without a care in the world for the ever-spreading pandemic.

Plenty of those present here would asymptomatically contract the virus and take it home to kill their parents, their grandparents, and more. But some, instead of doing that, would come home with her.

"We must all contribute to the war effort," she sighed, patriotically anticipating the devouring of fools.

13

RUNNING WILD

RAVEN CORINN CARLUK

Chastity rubbed at her neck, gaze darting towards the horizon. "We shouldn't do this. If the Alpha—"

Trevor laughed, pulling his shirt off. "How's the Alpha even gonna know? Ain't no one to see us." He sighed and stretched before pulling his pants off. "Better hurry, before you ruin that dress."

She shivered, fingering the neckline. "We're not supposed to change in the town."

Trevor cupped her cheeks and kissed her forehead. "It'll be fine. Just a quick run. No one's out to see us, so no one's out to be killed. Just two wolves enjoying the lack of people."

Sowing the Daemon Seed

HARI NAVARRO

Evil slouches before its blue-glow screen and caresses, urging the seed from the fruit it holds tight in the ball of its hand.

It smiles. "Finally, our epoch? How patiently our kind have bided the centuries, in wait of these—the very end of days."

Again, the masses lay plague upon themselves. "Again, with frothing lips they'll suckle at scripture and blame the fire-eyed ghoul. Soon now we will step upon the festered plains and claim this ruin entire. Evil is not immortal. We that are not bound to fantasy, arise!" spits this malignance who is nothing more than you.

CALLED TO DUTY

KIMBERLY REI

Time passed differently—more kindly—for Ted than for his human. He'd kept an eye on her since being set on the shelf so many years ago. It was his sworn duty to watch over her.

Now she was ill, and he could do nothing to help. His Suzie was coughing and writhing in her bed.

He pushed off the shelf, stretching plush limbs, flexing seams. He stood at the end of her bed.

He was only a bear, and maybe he couldn't protect her from a virus. But he could protect her from anything else that came her way.

BETTER ANGELS

NICOLA CURRIE

Two shifting columns appeared in a hospital ward, one black smoke, one white mist. The smoke twisted into a grinning red-eyed devil. The mist swirled into a kind face.

Dr Roberts and Nurse Emily awoke into the afterlife, the pandemic's newest victims.

Roberts cried in rage.

Emily never liked Roberts. He dismissed his patients' suffering, cared only for himself. Still, she felt his pain more than her own.

Roberts screamed as the devil of the smoke swallowed him whole.

The angel of the mist held Emily's hand.

"You are needed," she said, vanishing, watching invisibly as Emily resumed comforting, caring.

MOON 9

A Fae Wish Come True

J.W. GARRETT

Maya perked her ears—another intrusion. With a broad sweep of her wings, she barrelled down on the human who'd blundered into their land. Scrutinising the mortal, she gazed at three tiny stones that had gained him entrance. Sick, like others of his kind, the man should be ushered back to his world. Faeries weren't allowed to keep humans. But she had a special private collection. Lately, business was booming.

Working quickly, she fed him faerie food, ensuring his stay forever, covered him with illusion, then bound him with the other thirty sick specimens.

Now, back to slave number one…

13

DEATH TOLL

STACEY JAINE MCINTOSH

Puck rolled his eyes at the headline scrawling across the bottom of the tv screen: COVID-19 DEATH TOLL RISES!

He switched off the television with the remote before setting it down on the coffee table.

Humans were dropping like flies. Death gripped the urban landscape like the ice that encapsulated the Winter Court—his intended destination—but he'd lingered too long in the human realm, and now he was trapped in New York City.

But fey were immune.

"Gods above." Outside, while he gazed at the body bags piled three high, a tickle in his nose caused him to sneeze.

WARDED

STACEY JAINE MCINTOSH

The Winter Queen paced the confines of her sitting room. Rumours of a bad virus responsible for cutting down humans, swept Faerie. She worried what would happen if it took root within their borders.

Grimalkin darted in through the opened door before the attendants could close it on him.

"Well?" the Winter Queen demanded. "What's the latest?"

"Puck's trapped in the Summer Queen's apartment. Tam warded the borders before Puck could get out. It's spreading at an alarming rate."

"Find Tam. Get Puck out of there," she said. "Then have him seal the wards for good. Faerie is closed—forever!"

BLESSING IN DISGUISE

STACEY JAINE MCINTOSH

Tam Lin was the only fey gifted enough to break the wards in and out of Faerie. Right now, it was a blessing in disguise. The human world was chaos.

While the fey revelled in turning human lives upside down and inside out, they didn't relish death. And with the news reporting on how the dead would be buried off the coast on some island, Tam found himself relieved his race burned their dead. Ashes were much more civilised than bodies left to rot.

Or so he told himself as he worked into the night, sealing the borders of Faerie.

Taken Ill

STACEY JAINE MCINTOSH

Loose red curls spilled out over the white pillowcase. The Summer Queen had taken ill. Scarlett's body ached as her temperature soared. The common cold she thought she had, turned out to be far more dangerous.

"The test is positive," the doctor said. "It's Coronavirus, I'm sorry."

"She's a fighter." Worry furrowed the Summer King's brow. "She can beat this."

"That's the hope," the doctor turned her attention back to the Summer Queen. "Get some rest. You'll be feeling like your old self again in no time."

"I appreciate you taking the time. I just wish I shared your optimism."

13

STORM THE CASTLE

STACEY JAINE MCINTOSH

Whispers spread like wildfire. Rumours of the virus having crossed into Faerie from the human world despite heavy wards were rife.

The biggest rumour of all? That the Summer Queen was responsible for the transmission.

So, when it was confirmed the Queen was indeed a carrier, anarchy broke out.

Faeries came in droves to storm the castle, armed with sharp implements. Their goal? To bring down the Queen.

"Close the gates!" the guards cried. "Protect the Queen!"

"Kill the Queen!" the chorus of voices shouted.

Treason was punishable by death, meted out by the virus that would decimate the crowd.

The Culling

G. ALLEN WILBANKS

"Is it The Culling?"

"We are not sure, Bright Lady," the elf admitted, bowing deeply before his queen. "The humans have abandoned the forests and withdrawn into their homes, but their numbers have not significantly reduced."

The queen's hands clenched into delicate fists and her features hardened in decision.

"Our domain dwindles. The days of hiding and waiting for succor are at an end. If this disease is not The Culling we had hoped for, mayhap it will still be an opportunity for more direct action."

"Go and spread the word," she directed the elf. "The Fae are at war!"

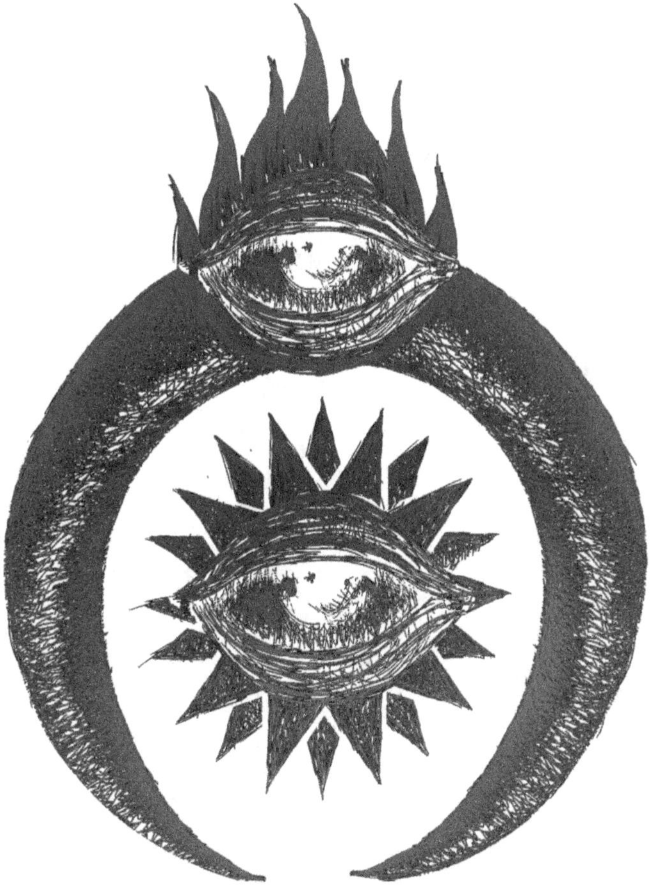

MOON 10

The Ghosts of Juniper Lane

NICOLE LITTLE

"Why's it always freezing here?!"

"We bought a fixer-upper, Freddie. It's drafty."

"And those godawful noises this morning? I almost miss going into work!"

***

"How much longer can we keep this up?" Eloise complained. "They *never* leave anymore. We deserve a break!"

Primrose nodded, agreeing. She eased shut the bedroom door, waiting for the screech of rusty hinges. Then she slammed it.

***

"You hear that?!"

Cassidy rolled her eyes. "Time for a walk! You need to get out for a bit."

As the couple exited, the exhausted ghosts of the haunted house on Juniper Lane moaned a sigh of relief.

A Red Feast

J.W. GARRETT

Drake rose from his coffin, his appetite whetted for another busy night. Lines had formed in their dank basement while he'd slept. Each day outpaced the last. When the first tints of orange signalled dawn, the remaining humans were sent away to try again another day.

With the advent of the newest virus haunting their kind, humans' fragile reality had shifted. Some hunted for meat and toilet paper with primal instincts as strong as the vampires who sought blood.

Once turned, the undead humans wouldn't succumb to the dreaded illness. Sinking his fangs into the first, he feasted.

"Mmm. Next!"

SELF DEFENCE

DAVID GREEN

They invaded Earth at its weakest.

Covid-19 destroyed our infrastructure, our economy; forced us to separate so we couldn't rally a fight back.

Goddamn aliens from outer space. Who'd have believed it?

It took them a matter of days to defeat us. Still, they were curious. Enjoyed asking us questions in between their experiments and told us of their home planet. They didn't have pollution or disease—they'd attacked us as a preemptive strike.

Fifteen days after they arrived, they started to die.

Covid-19 hit humans hard.

But for a species that hadn't dealt with disease, it killed without mercy.

13

MILES TO GO

KIMBERLY REI

It was getting harder to breathe. Medical staff hustled in and out of the room, doing their best for her. Sara was scared, but she knew she had to stay calm and let them do their work.

The voice told her so.

It had been there since before the outbreak, a soft whispering, seductive in her dreams. Sometimes, she saw it, the owner of the voice. It was a beautiful creature, with flames for hair and sin for eyes.

She gasped, panic rising.

The voice returned, smiling. "Oh no, Sara, we're not giving up. We have too much work to do."

The First Zombie

HARI NAVARRO

Dead, aren't I?

But then, it only eats the elderly, right?

The compromised. The weak.

I was careful. Washed my fucking hands, stayed at home.

Drowning in cold, floundering, fingers numb.

She was my neighbour. Saw her before the lockdown, we never talked. Bobbed hair, smells like vanilla.

Fuck.

I licked her, and the virus licked me back. We joked about Romero and Kirkman's undead wanderers.

Cold. That's what they say, right?

Cold, so very cold.

Back of useless knuckles rap upon my casket ceiling.

Time?

Lost, but I'm thinking I've been here a while.

A very, very long while.

A New Reign

MCKENZIE RICHARDSON

They'd been used to the constant noise; shuffling feet, muffled voices, hammering, pounding. It was the silence that woke them.

They shook their massive heads, one and then the other. Twin necks stretched long to rid themselves of aches, scales catching where they met just above the shared body.

With snarled claws, lengthy with disuse, they tunneled to the surface. After centuries of sleep, the sun was blinding, but when their eyes adjusted, colossal teeth gleamed in a pair of reptilian smiles.

No humans walked the streets. The world was ready for the taking.

The dragons would soon reign again.

A Smorgasbord in Perpetual Slumber

TERRY MILLER

Three times the rooster crowed, but no one on the farm rose for the new day. The early morning sun peeked through the windows, illuminating the stillness inside the house. Mr and Mrs Tucker lay quiet in their bed. Mrs Tucker was the first to go, gasping for her last breaths. Mr Tucker followed suit, content in his fateful, perpetual slumber.

Maggots crawled, parting the wrinkles in thin skin. They burrowed deep, satiating their hunger in the fresh smorgasbord before them.

A grey figure patiently watched at their upstairs bedroom window, returning each morning as the Tuckers withered to bones.

MOON II

13

The Cost of Vanity

DAVID GREEN

Maeve saw no way of escaping the rut she was in.

A Leannan Sidhe, Meave lengthened her years by stealing the vitality of others. The fae inspired creative souls to achieve something wonderful and extracted her price in return.

The 21st century proved fruitful. Writers, begging for a muse, crammed into coffee shops.

Maeve played the part, but now the humans hid in their homes. Those venturing out wouldn't come close enough for her glamour to work.

Maeve cried as she stared into her mirror. An ancient face wept back. The stolen years had caught up, and that wouldn't do.

13

OVERHEATED

KIMBERLY REI

On the run. Out of time.

Until now, he'd remained hidden with ease. Now the humans had some sort of disease making them paranoid. Tomak hissed, gills under his shirt fluttering in irritation. His body heat wasn't considered "normal" among the two-legs. His glamour implant managed everything else, but these random tests would mark him, and then he'd be screwed.

For decades, he'd avoided capture, staying indoors and shielded from scans. The virus forced him out in the open.

With predatory stealth, the shadow was upon him. One flaring burst and Tomak burst into flames. His people had no mercy.

The Remains of the Day

J.W. GARRETT

The alien spacecraft maintained orbit around Earth, awaiting orders to proceed. The final action had been approved. Invasion timeline set. Earth was to be under their control. One week in human terms was all they'd need.

Then the culling could begin. Turn humans with the most potential. Put others to work cleaning the wasteland of debris. Some weren't salvageable.

Then, when mass chaos ensued, consuming the planet, unlike anything seen during the ten year observation period, the council reconsidered. Apparently, human's capacity for adaptation and rational thought had been grossly overstated.

"Confirm?"

"Negative. Clear the surface for habitation. Leave none."

Pandemic Market Western

J.M. Meyer

Jittery, I adjust my mask and play a favourite R.E.M. song on my headphones. The sounds of rattling carts, loud voices and coughing disappear. I pile into the local market with other panic buyers. I need one important item. A surreal opera plays before me: empty shelves, overflowing carts, worried faces. I peer down my desired aisle and spy one lone bag and it's my *Precious*. At the end of the empty lane stands a demon eyeing it, too. We pause, like gunslingers, before sprinting; each grabbing the necessity. The Hershey bars rain down. Nothing a little sanitiser can't fix.

Haunted Love

K.R. NOX

Matthew sighed. The Covid-19 Lockdown was grating on his nerves. He wanted to go back to work, go for a drink with friends, and get outdoors again. His house was beginning to feel like a prison.

Sitting in his home office it went suddenly cold. He stiffened, looking about. "I'm going mad," he muttered to himself.

***

Katherine watched Matthew longingly. He couldn't see her, couldn't touch her…didn't know she existed—yet she was happy. The vicious pandemic ravaging the world meant she got to see him more often.

She sighed, unconsciously toying with the gaping bullet wound in her head.

Means to an End

D. KERSHAW

He awoke from fevered dreams; damp hair, gasping breaths, flushing heat. Fading memories—bare skin, soft touches—sparked the periphery of his consciousness as cold fingers caressed his cheek, icy breath whispered his name.

He *knew* she was real, not a figment. She filled his empty life—devoid of contact, work, friends, for months—every sleeping and waking moment. He was wonting. *Obsessed.*

Needed her…to be *with* her.

And it was too easy. The unmasked cougher in the supermarket. Touch what he touched.

And now he waits—gasping breaths, flushing heat, cold hands on hot cheeks—for the end.

13
NEVER ALONE

K.R. NOX

Katherine sat on Matthew's bed as he struggled to breathe. He was deteriorating rapidly, his lungs filling with fluid. "It's going to be alright," she said, stroking his feverish forehead. "I watch your television news. You're going to drown soon, but I'll be here. We can be together."

***

Matthew felt a ghostly coolness temporarily relieve the fire of COVID-19. All night he fought, his phone beyond reach. When, finally, he breathed his last, he sat up—outside himself.

"A bullet would have been kinder."

He stared in shock at the young green-eyed woman in Victorian period clothing seated beside him.

MOON 12

A NEW RACE WILL RISE

TERRY MILLER

"The humans that contract and survive this virus will move to the next testing phase." The charismatic scientist addressed his colleagues. "We will implement the gestation phase in the coming months."

The DNA research was promising and imperative for the development of a species capable of surviving the Earth's atmosphere. The alien strain would prove dominant during the pubescent years, the physical traits becoming more profound.

"A new race will rise from the demise of two; the future is here."

The Class B Research Vessel erupted with joyful praise as the first of the viral delivery systems breached the atmosphere.

13

WITCHES BREW

J.W. GARRETT

The coven stared at the men in their midst. Government officials here for treatment against humanity's latest illness? As they'd left, Beatrix muttered a spell, shrouding their location from the mortals. Immune due to the magic pumping through their veins, witches could offer a vaccine, but with discretion. Covens around the world wouldn't go back to a time when they were hunted, then burned at the stake.

The one official remaining shuddered. Only a down payment, he would do for now. Beatrix's knife gleamed in the air before slicing across his wrist. Hooded beings chanted, united in the blood sacrifice.

WALPURGIS

J.M. AMES

They did it to themselves, we cleaned up after. The first viral wave wasn't too deadly, because most stayed indoors—at first. Then, as always, the humans got greedy, and came out early. That's when the second wave hit. Took about 20% of the population before they went back into their homes. On the night of April 30th, we landed our ships and began operations. Most stayed in their homes, unaware neighbours were disappearing. Once some figured it out, it was too late. Few escaped into spaceships, and one detonated Purple Haze, ending all remaining life on the planet.

Four Brothers

K.B. ELIJAH

"It was good when the panic buying started," my brother complained, eyeing the plate of doughnuts with a feverish look. "But now everyone is binge-eating!"

The man to his right slammed a meaty fist onto the table. "I thought we agreed the twenty-first century was meant to be mine, brother!"

My other sibling just shrugged, reaching for a doughnut. "You had most of the twentieth."

I raised an eyebrow. "You're not going to whinge at me too?"

Death looked up, his amused mouth laced with icing. "Oh, absolutely. Pick your game up, Pestilence: the fatality rate is *far* too low."

Clear Skies

RAVEN CORINN CARLUK

Thunderbird stirred in her prison, testing her bonds, finding new weaknesses. Escape was no longer merely a goal for the rekindled god; it was an inevitability.

For a century and a half, she'd lain awake, unable to rise from cold iron bonds. Humans called them railways, but few had seen the sigils used to keep her underground.

The rails had declined over time, but trains had been replaced by metal birds and trails of chemical. Thunderbird could not escape those either, only wear at the ethereal walls.

But the metal birds were less frequent. The sigils failed, and Thunderbird stirred.

Safety First

G. ALLEN WILBANKS

He spoke the final words of the incantation. The candles at each point of the pentagram flared, creating a smoke that slowly coalesced into a solid form.

The new figure in the summoning circle gazed at him, calmly. She was tall, voluptuous, and quite naked.

"I've called you here, Succubus, and I compel you to do my bidding!" he ordered the sultry demon.

"Of course, Master," she purred. "I am happy to do anything you wish. Might I make one request, however?"

She held up a small cloth item in her hand: A surgical mask.

"Do you mind wearing this?"

Unlocked

XIMENA ESCOBAR

They know not to go to certain places. Not to feed certain appetites. Once you unlock certain doors, there's no turning back. Or, there's no stopping whatever comes.

But now everything's shut, there's not much else to do.

People have long carried the keys, but distraction is scarce like flour these days and they can't ignore the clinking anymore, in the deafening silence of empty cities and pockets. Keeping them awake as they bury their heads under their pillows, trying to ignore the knocking.

Trying to supress the urges…

"For Satan finds some mischief still for idle hands to do."

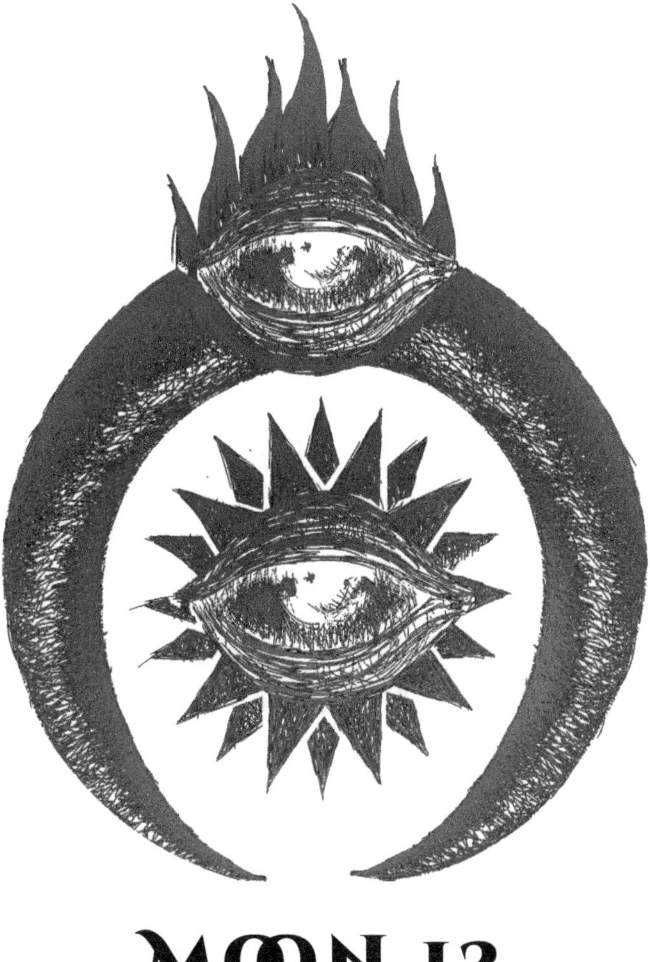

MOON 13

STAY THE FUCK AT HOME

D. KERSHAW

Noise woke him. He scowled into the darkness.

"There's nothing oooooon!" whined a voice.

"There's lots," said another.

"I've watched *all* of Netflix."

"All?"

"Allllllllll!"

"It's my turn to choose," interrupted a third. "Ru Paul's Drag Race!"

"No!" chorused the others.

Jeremiah rose—his feet left no prints in the dust—and transcended from attic to lounge.

The Grant family fled in fear, screams echoing.

***

Shouting woke him. He scowled into the darkness.

Jeremiah rose—no breath parted cobwebs—and transcended from attic to lounge.

"Don't scowl, Jeremiah," said Mrs Grant, her spectral form shimmering. "It's your fault we're here."

Captain Armchair

NICOLE LITTLE

Pale light illuminates the ruggedly handsome features of our caped crusader, our fearless hero in blue tights; his keen eye shrewdly searches and seeks. What brings him here in the dead of night? Will he foil a daring robbery or rescue a damsel in distress? He's the fastest, the strongest ... the bravest of the brave.

Record scratch

Freeze frame

"Oh, come *on*! I'm just trying to get a drink here! All the bad guys are staying home. So am I! Give me a break!"

He grabs a beer and slams the refrigerator door, plunging the kitchen back into darkness.

Going Hungry

GALINA TREFIL

Lethargic and pale, the vampire wandered the empty Italian streets. *Damn it.* He scowled; he couldn't go on much longer like this. He needed blood.

And then he saw her. Oh, she was perfect. Well, no…not really perfect…but she was alive and in front of him, and pandemics created low standards. He beckoned her forward. "Where do you think you're going?" he purred hypnotically.

"I'm donating plasma. I recovered from Covid-19."

The ever-so-famished vampire stopped. Desperately, he wanted the world, and his regular menu, to return to normal. So, he fled before his hunger overtook his better judgement.

Witch's Brew

NICOLA CURRIE

My neighbour Tom is a man of science. He was quick to tell me so, knocking on my door that first time, telling me he was complaining to the council about the smell of my restoring teas, ancient remedies, medicinal herbs.

I tolerated it until he got other residents involved, complained to the local press, branded me unintelligent, charlatan, make-believer.

Funny. He believes now, banging on my door, red-faced from coughing, seeking comfort when his science has none.

I never meant things to get so out of control. Oh, well. I sip my tea, guarding the solution in cupped hands.

The Ghost That Pushes You Down

MCKENZIE RICHARDSON

Samnang awoke to a tingling in his spine, sensing another presence in the room.

Nearly blending in with the blackness, an inky shape advanced.

As it drew near his bed, Samnang was sure it was simply a trick of the light.

But there was no mistaking the icy hand that pressed upon his chest. His lungs tightened, seizing up as it became harder to breathe.

His soul slipped off in the shadow-demon's hand as easily as shedding clothes.

Silently, the *khmaoch sângkât* melted into the night.

So many humans confined to their homes made it much simpler to collect souls.

The Tangerine Shower

HARI NAVARRO

The End?

Father sought guidance. The soothsaying Delphi bitch, the five dollar reading. Foretold; my offspring would incite the mortals to suckle of his throbbing nipple, thus ushering in the end.

Father's weakness was humanity, so he locked my virgin ass up in a chamber of bronze, shitty turd place bronze.

Great Zeus—who, turns out, kind of fancied me—appeared as orange rain. Streaming through the bars and down into my womb.

Across the Covid decimation, I see my boy all grown up. Such pride as he puffs out his tangerine chest and offers the baying masses a sip.

The Breath of Fey

XIMENA ESCOBAR

The puff isn't a single flower, but a cluster of tiny florets, each producing a single seed. Broken apart by an Earth Fairy's whisper, they fly like spinning ballerinas, gliding down and slithering into unknowing cavities. The explosion blossoms silently, but loss is loud and so is fear.

Surrounded by walls and distance, humans feel safer. They don't understand how debilitating fear is. It filters through computer screens like water through paper.

They don't realise we aren't concerned with the survival of the individual but only with that of the species.

The strong will remain, and the species will thrive.

Author Biographies

DAVID GREEN grew up between Manchester, UK and Galway, Ireland. A reader from an early age, David had long harboured dreams of writing himself. Throwing himself into any genre, David enjoys creating breathing characters to challenge—and finds horror a wonderfully terrifying space to work in. Twitter: @davidpgreen83

D. KERSHAW is co-founder and editor of Black Hare Press. Having found that his degrees were as useful in real life as calculus and geometric proofs, Dean now works in commercial non-fiction during the day and moonlights as a minion of the hell hare, Captain Woundwort, in the dark hours. You'll usually find him hanging out with the rest of the BHP family in the BHP Facebook group.

E.L. GILES is a dreamer, passionate about art, a restless worker and a bit of a weird human. He started his artistic journey as a music composer until the need to put his thoughts and stories down on paper grew too strong for him to resist it any longer. He lives in the French Province of Quebec, Canada, with his girlfriend and two boys.
Facebook: elgilesauthor
Website: www.elgilesauthor.com

G. ALLEN WILBANKS is a member of the Horror Writers Association (HWA) and has published over 100 short stories in various magazines and on-line venues. He is the author of two short story collections, and the novel, When Darkness Comes.
Website: www.gallenwilbanks.com
Blog: DeepDarkThoughts.com

GALINA TREFIL is a novelist specializing in women's, minority, and disabled rights. Her favourite genres are horror, thriller, and historical fiction. Her short stories and articles have appeared in Neurology Now, UnBound Emagazine, The Guardian, Tikkun, Romea.CZ, Jewcy, Jewrotica, Telegram Magazine, Ink Drift Magazine, The Dissident Voice, Open Road Review, and the anthologies "Flock: The Journey," "First Love," "Sea of Secrets," "Coffins and Dragons," "Organic Ink volume One," "Winds of Despair," "Waters of Destruction," "Curses & Cauldrons," "Unravel," "Hate," "Love," "Oceans," "Forgotten Ones," "Dark Valentine Holiday Horror Collection," and "Suspense Unimagined."
Website: galinatrefil.wordpress.com
Facebook: Rabbi-Galina-Trefil-535886443115467

HARI NAVARRO has, for many years now, been locked in his neighbour's cellar. He survives due to an intravenous feed of puréed extreme horror and Absinthe infused sticky-spiced unicorn wings. His anguished cries for help can be found via 365 Tomorrows, Breachzine, AntipodeanSF, Horror Without Borders, Black Hare Press and HellBound books. Hari was the Winner of the Australasian Horror Writers' Association Flash Fiction Award 2018 and has also succeeded in being a New Zealander who now lives in Northern Italy with no cats.
Amazon: amazon.com/Hari-Navarro
Tumblr: harinavarro.tumblr.com/

J.M. AMES is an award-winning multi-genre speculative fiction author native to Southern California. He has multiple short story publications dating back to 2016. One thing holds true throughout all of his stories - you can Expect the Unexpected.
When not working his day job or enjoying his fatherly adventures, he writes short stories and novels, including an upcoming series. You can follow him on a variety of platforms, details on his website.
Website: jm-ames.com/contact-jm/

J.M. MEYER is a writer, artist and small business owner living in New York, where she received her master's degree from Teachers College, Columbia University. Jacqueline enjoys writing speculative fiction and mysteries. Her favorite author is Alice Munro and her favorite film…is…anything horror related. Jacqueline also enjoys hiking with her dog Molly and the company of her husband Bruce and daughters; Julia, Emma and Lauren. Jacqueline's Mantra lately; there's no such thing as failing, it's called learning.
Website: jmoranmeyer.net
Amazon: amazon.com/author/jacquelinemoranmeyer

J.W. GARRETT has been writing in one form or another since she was a teenager. She currently lives in Florida with her family but loves the mountains of Virginia where she was born. Her writings include YA fantasy as well as short stories. Since completing Remeon's Quest-Earth Year 1930, the prequel in her YA fantasy series, Realms of Chaos, she has been hard at work on the next in the series, scheduled to release August 2020. When she's not hanging out with her characters, her favourite activities are reading, running and spending time with family.
Website: www.jwgarrett.com
BHC Press: www.bhcpress.com/Author_JW_Garrett.html

JODI JENSEN, author of time travel romances and speculative fiction short stories, grew up moving from California, to Massachusetts, and a few other places in between, before finally settling in Utah at the ripe old age of nine. The nomadic life fed her sense of adventure as a child and the wanderlust continues to this day. With a passion for old cemeteries, historical buildings and sweeping sagas of days gone by, it was only natural she'd dream of time traveling to all the places that sparked her imagination.
Twitter: @WritesJodi
Facebook: jodijensenwrites

K.B. ELIJAH is a fantasy author living in Brisbane, Australia with her husband and three cockatiels. A lawyer by day, and a writer by...also day, because she needs her solid nine hours of sleep per night (not that the cockatiels let her sleep past 6am). K.B. writes for various international anthologies, and her work features in dozens of collections about the mysterious, the magical and the macabre. Her own books of short fantasy novellas with twists, The Empty Sky and Out of the Nowhere, are available on paperback and Kindle now.
Website: www.kbelijah.com
Instagram: k.b.elijah

K.R. NOX is a Western Australian poet, and short story writer. Being a consummate lover of ancient myths and legends, the occult, and all things dark and erotic, means there is always something deliciously creative brewing on the horizon...
Website: www.krnox.com

KIMBERLY REI has been writing for as long as she can remember. At five years old, her parents gifted her with a set of Children's Classics that she had no hope of reading. Yet. The potential alone sparked a love of words that has never wavered. Kim has taught writing workshops and edited novels for Authors You May Recognize. She has published several short stories and now can't stop chasing paper dragons. She currently lives in Tampa Bay, Florida with her wife and an abundance of gorgeous beaches to explore.

MCKENZIE RICHARDSON lives in Milwaukee, WI. Her horror stories have been featured in various anthologies including Evil Lurks, Pandemic, and After: Undead Wars. She has also published a variety of poems and flash fiction pieces.
Facebook: mckenzielrichardson
Blog: www.craft-cycle.com

NICOLA CURRIE is from Cambridge, UK where she works in educational publishing. She has published poetry in literary magazines, including Mslexia and Sarasvati, and short stories in various anthologies. She has also completed her first novel, which was longlisted for the Bath Children's Novel Award.
Website: writeitandweep.home.blog

NICOLE LITTLE is an award winning short story writer living in St. John's, Newfoundland, Canada. Her publishing credits include Sweet Sixteen (Kit Sora: The Artobiography, 2019), The Market and Last One Standing (Dystopia from the Rock, 2019); Far Out and On a Wing and a Prayer (Flights from the Rock, 2019). Her short story Doxxed placed favorably in the Writers Alliance of Newfoundland and Labrador's "A Nightmare on Water Street: Scary Story Reading". In her spare time, Nicole can be found with either a pen in her hand or her nose in a book. She is married with two daughters.

RAVEN CORINN CARLUK writes dark fantasy, paranormal romance, and anything else that catches her interest. She's authored five novels, where she explores themes of love and acceptance. Her shorter pieces, usually from her darker side, can be found in Black Hare Press anthologies, at Detritus Online, and through Alban Lake Publishers.
Twitter: @ravencorinn
Website: www.ravencorinncarluk.com

STACEY JAINE MCINTOSH was born in Perth, Western Australia where she still resides with her husband and their four children. Although her first love has always been writing, she once toyed with being a Cartographer and subsequently holds a Diploma in Spatial Information Services. Since 2011, she has had a vast number of stories and a few poems published online as well as in various anthologies. Stacey is also the author of Solstice, Morrighan, Lost and Le Fay and she is currently working on several other projects simultaneously. When not with her family or writing she enjoys reading, photography, genealogy, history, Arthurian myths and witchcraft.
Website: www.staceyjainemcintosh.com

TERRY MILLER lives in Portsmouth, Ohio. His work has been featured in Sanitarium Magazine, Devolution Z, Jitter, Rhysling Anthology 2017, Poetry Quarterly, Sirens Call Ezine, The Horror Tree's Trembling With Fear, SpillWords, Organic Ink Vol. I, Curses & Cauldrons Anthology from Blood Song Books, Forest of Fear from Blood Song Books, the Dark Drabble Anthology Series from Black Hare Press, 100 Word Zombie Bites from Reanimated Writers Press, Scary Snippets, Guilty Pleasures & Other Dark Delights, 100 Word Horrors 3, and O Unholy Night In Deathlehem from Grinning Skull Press.
Facebook: tmiller2015
Amazon: amazon.com/author/millerterryl

XIMENA ESCOBAR is writing stories and poetry. Originally from Chile, she is the author of a translation into Spanish of the Broadway Musical "The Wizard of Oz", and of an original adaptation of the same, "Navidad en Oz", both produced in her home country. Since 2018 she has published several short stories in various anthologies and online platforms, and is now slowly working on her own collection. Ximena has a degree in Arts & Communication Science and lives in Nottingham with her family.
Facebook: Ximenautora
Twitter: @laximenin

ZOEY XOLTON is an Australian Speculative Fiction writer, primarily of Dark Fantasy, Paranormal Romance and Horror. She is also a proud mother of two and is married to her soul mate. Outside of her family, writing is her greatest passion. She is especially fond of short fiction and is working on releasing her own themed collections in future.
Website: www.zoeyxolton.com

ABOUT THE PUBLISHER

BLACK HARE PRESS is a small, independent publisher based in Melbourne, Australia.

Founded in 2018, our aim has always been to champion emerging authors from all around the globe and offer opportunities for them to participate in speculative fiction and horror short story anthologies.

www.blackharepress.com

13

www.ingramcontent.com/pod-product-compliance
Lightning Source LLC
LaVergne TN
LVHW012210070526
838202LV00027B/2633/J